Ella on Her Own

A Fairy Tale

retold by Linda Yoshizawa
illustrated by Sheila Bailey

MODERN CURRICULUM PRESS

Pearson Learning Group

Dear Diary,

Today I started my summer job. I'm a helper for a family in the city. It wasn't what I expected. The girls in the family are rude and messy. They spent the day watching TV and talking on the phone. Then they went shopping. When they came home, they whirled around in their new clothes. They told each other how good they looked. But they didn't look good. After all, beauty *is* as beauty *does*.

Dear Diary,

This job isn't getting any better. I get no free time. I never get to read. I don't have time to make friends. I just work all day long. I wash and iron all the clothes. Then I clean everyone's room. By dinner time, I look so tired and dirty that the family makes fun of me. My name is Elli—with an *i*. But they call me Cinderella.

I've got to find a better job!

Dear Diary,

   Those girls were on the phone all day again today. This time they really had something to talk about. An invitation came in the mail. The mayor is giving a ball for her son. Everyone in the city is invited.

   That means I'm invited too. Maybe—just maybe—I'll make some friends. Maybe I'll meet the mayor's son. Or maybe I'll meet someone who will give me a new job.

Dear Diary,

Bad, bad news! I can't go to the ball after all.

My boss even laughed when I asked her. "You?" she sneered. "You'll have to work overtime. You'll be busy helping the girls and me get ready. You won't have time to get yourself ready for a ball."

I'm so sad I could cry.

Dear Diary,

I keep thinking how awful I'll feel if I don't get to go to the ball. I'd be scrubbing, as usual. And I'd have to pretend that those girls look great. No way! I won't give up. I *will* find a way to go to the ball.

Dear Diary,

The ball is tomorrow. I still don't have anything to wear. I haven't been able to find a minute to sneak away to shop. Once upon a time, someone kind and wonderful would have appeared. She'd just wink or blink, and there I'd be in a beautiful gown. But those kinds of things just don't happen anymore.

Dear Diary,

I don't need any help after all! Today I snatched up some catalogs that came in the mail. I found a beautiful gown. I found some great shoes too. They're made of glass. No one else will have anything like them. I ordered everything by computer, and the package will be shipped overnight. I just have to get to it first. Thank goodness I saved my money to pay for these things!

Dear Diary,

I'm writing this as I wait for my cab. I wasn't sure I'd make it. I worked hard all day. Then I was busy trying to make everyone in the family look beautiful. It didn't help much, though. Luckily, I can get ready in a hurry. I'm putting on the gown and my fancy glass slippers and going off to the ball! I'll write more, Dear Diary, when I get home.

Well, Dear Diary, the mayor really knows how to throw a party! Her son was so handsome. Of course, I was late, but he saw me as soon as I walked in. In fact, everyone's head whipped around as I came through the door. I looked so good that no one recognized me. Later I whirled and whirled around the dance floor. The mayor's son really seemed to like me!

Suddenly I saw my grumpy boss and her daughters walking to the door. Oh, no! I had to beat them home!

I ran to a cab. The mayor's son ran after me, but there was no time to explain. Just before I hopped into the cab, I tripped. Of all the times to stumble, I had to stumble then! I lost one of my fancy slippers. I couldn't even stop to pick it up.

Dear Diary,

   Today everyone is talking about the ball.
The biggest news is that the mayor's son
snatched up a glass slipper after the ball.
He wants to find the girl who wore it.
That's me! He's going to visit every house.
All the women will try on the slipper.

   There's the doorbell. I'll be back!

Dear Diary,

You won't believe what happened! Just as the glass slipper was on my foot, it fell. Crash! The slipper broke into a thousand pieces. Guess who had to clean up all that sharp glass!

I could have shown him the other glass slipper. But the whole thing gave me a better idea.

Plastic slippers!

They're unbreakable!